Red Fox at Hickory Lane

SMITHSONIAN'S BACKYARD

To Jean Connors, for stepping in, for staying there . . . for everything. — K.H.

This art is dedicated to education, public concern and all efforts to protect the diversity of life on Earth. — W.S.

Book design: Shields & Partners, Westport, CT
Book layout: Marcin D. Pilchowski
Editor: Laura Gates Galvin
Editorial assistance: Chelsea Shriver

First Edition 2004
10 9 8 7 6 5 4 3 2 1
Printed in Singapore

Acknowledgements
　　Our very special thanks to Dr. Richard W. Thorington, Jr., Curator of Mammals, Department of Zoology, National Museum of Natural History.
　　Soundprints would like to thank Ellen Nanney and Katie Mann at the Smithsonian Institution's Office of Product Development and Licensing for their help in the creation of this book.

Library of Congress Cataloging-in-Publication Data

Hollenback, Kathleen M.
　　Red Fox at Hickory Lane / by Kathleen M. Hollenbeck ; illustrated by Wendy Smith..-- 1st ed.
　　　p. cm. -- (Smithsonian's backyard)
　　Summary: Father Fox and Mother Fox care for their four cubs in a den near Hickory Lane.
　　Includes notes on the red fox.
　　ISBN 1-59249-113-8 (hardcover) -- ISBN 1-59249-114-6 (micro hbk) -- ISBN 1-59249-115-4 (pbk.)
　　　1. Red Fox--Juvenile fiction. [1. Red fox—Fiction.] I. Smith, Wendy, ill. II. Title. III. Series.

PZ10.3.H716Re 2003
[E]—dc21
　　　　　　　　　　　　　　　　　　　　　　　2003050368

Red Fox at Hickory Lane

by Kathleen M. Hollenbeck

Illustrated by Wendy Smith

Soundprints

Where Children Discover...

It is early evening in the backyard of the yellow house on Hickory Lane. The warm summer sun has just slipped out of sight.

Crouched in the shadows at the foot of a tree, a father red fox waits.

A young mouse scurries through the grass nearby.
Ears perked, Father Fox remains quiet and still.
He cannot see the mouse, but he can hear it.
Father Fox crouches lower and then leaps
from his hiding place. He pounces on the
unsuspecting mouse and traps it beneath
his front paws.

Carrying the mouse in his mouth, Father Fox trots to
the edge of the backyard. He slips through a hole between
two bushes and disappears into the woods.

Skillfully, Father Fox makes his own path through the trees.
His footsteps are sure and silent. He comes to a clearing and stops,
dropping the mouse beside a tall fern.

Father Fox pushes the fern aside to reveal a hole in the ground. Once the home of a woodchuck, it is now a fox den. Father Fox waits by the den. He watches as Mother Fox climbs out.

Seconds later, four furry cubs scurry out of the den and into the moonlight. One sees the mouse and grabs it with his mouth. As he eats it, the other cubs rush to Father Fox. He opens his mouth and lets the cubs sniff inside. Finding no food there, they begin to play.

Father Fox and Mother Fox sit in the clearing and watch their cubs. The cubs chase each other. They tumble in the low grass and pounce. They wrestle and fight. Such play helps the cubs grow stronger. It teaches them skills they will need to survive on their own.

The cubs practice hunting, too. They pounce on beetles and grasshoppers. They play with feathers and sticks that Mother Fox brought from the woods. They use them as toys for chewing and pouncing.

A leaf scrapes across the ground. Last month, this noise would have scared the cubs back into the den. Today, they are stronger and braver. They ignore it.

Later, Father Fox and Mother Fox hunt together in the woods around the den. Father Fox sniffs. He senses a rabbit nearby. He crouches on one side of a thicket. Then he lunges, scaring the rabbit from its resting place.

The rabbit leaps out of the thicket, straight into the path of Mother Fox. In a flash, Mother Fox pounces and catches the rabbit in her mouth.

Father Fox and Mother Fox lead their cubs on a short trip into the woods. They teach them to hunt for food such as berries, insects, and earthworms.

There is much the cubs need to learn as they grow. On later trips, their parents will teach them how to catch prey, find safe spots to rest, store food, and avoid danger.

As the family hunts, Father Fox sees a coyote among the trees. He barks, warning Mother Fox and the cubs that danger is near. Father Fox slowly trots away in full view of the coyote! The coyote chases Father Fox through the woods.

Mother Fox quickly leads her cubs to safety in a nearby woodchuck burrow.

The coyote is fast, but Father Fox outruns him. The coyote turns around and approaches the woodchuck burrow where Mother Fox and the cubs are hiding. He sticks his nose in and sniffs. The opening is too small, and he can't reach Mother Fox and the cubs. Defeated, the coyote slowly walks away.

Dawn is near. Mother Fox and her cubs return to their den in the woods. The cubs are tired from their play and the exciting hunting trip. They stretch out lazily in front of the den. Mother Fox lies down to keep watch.

As the sun rises, Father Fox returns to the backyard behind the yellow house.

By autumn, the cubs will no longer need Father Fox. They will be nearly full grown and will leave their den to find homes of their own.

Like their father, they will find food and teach their own cubs to hunt. Until then, Father Fox will continue the life he knows — spending nights with the cubs and days on his own, behind the yellow house on Hickory Lane.

About the Red Fox

The red fox lives throughout most of North America, Europe, Asia, and in parts of northern Africa, India, and Japan. A member of the canine family, the red fox weighs about as much as a small dog. Its distinctive, bushy tail nearly matches the length of its body.

Despite its name, a red fox may have reddish-brown, silver, or black fur. By six months of age, its thick fur coat has two layers: one to protect the animal from wind and water and one to keep its body warm.

When threatened, red foxes most often avoid danger by running away, unless they have offspring in tow. Sure-footed, swift, and intelligent, they are known to lead predators on a wild chase through brush and bramble, over fallen trees and across streams. Usually successful in outwitting predators, the red fox is often aptly labeled sly and crafty.

Glossary

clearing: An area of forest that is free of trees.
coyote: An animal that is a member of the dog family
 and is larger than a fox and smaller than a wolf.

pounce: To jump on something suddenly and hold it.
scurry: To run with short, quick steps.
woodchuck: A very large ground squirrel that makes large burrows.

Points of Interest in This Book

pp. 10-11: fox den, mother fox (vixen)
pp. 12-13: fox cubs check parent's
 mouth for food.
pp. 18-19: parents work as pair to trap prey.
pp. 20-21: cubs learn to find food, catch prey,
 find safe spots to rest, store food.

pp. 22-23: coyote threatens.
pp. 24-25: foxes fight to protect territory.
pp. 28-29: fox cubs grow nearly full-size
 in first six months
pp. 30-31: foxes sleep by day and hunt at night

6/05